This Little Hippo
book belongs to

Gabry Book

07751

For Jo, Mark, Katie and Amie

Scholastic Children's Books,
Commonwealth House, 1-19 New Oxford Street,
London WC1A 1NU, UK
a division of Scholastic Ltd

London • New York • Toronto • Sydney • Auckland

First published in the UK in 1997 by Little Hippo,
an imprint of Scholastic Ltd

Copyright © Peter Kavanagh, 1997

ISBN 0 590 19455 0

Printed and bound in Spain by G.Z. Printek

The Three Little Guinea Pigs

Written and Illustrated by

Peter Kavanagh

Little Hippo

Once there were three great friends
called Molly, Jolly and Polly.

They all lived in Mr Jones' petshop
and they loved playing together.

All day long, they chased and tumbled
and burrowed and bustled around the
other guinea pigs.

And at night, they snuggled and
snored together in a cosy heap.

They were very happy in the petshop,
but they had one great fear . . .
customers.

Sometimes people came and stared
and sometimes a guinea pig was
taken away forever.

The three friends were afraid that one day somebody would buy one of them and take them away.

So they pretended to be dull and boring, to trick customers into choosing other guinea pigs and not them.

If this didn't work, they nipped
Mr Jones' finger. That always
frightened the customers away!

And so the three friends went along,
until one rainy Saturday morning . . .

Molly was playing
with the food bowl
and didn't notice
the little girl, until
it was too late.
"That one,
please, Dad."

Molly tried to look fierce, but the
little girl wouldn't have any other.
Then Mr Jones put the heavy gloves on.

Jolly and Polly watched
in horror, as Molly was
lifted away from them
and put into a box.

The little girl and her Mum and Dad left the shop. Molly was gone forever.

Molly felt very lost. She was put into
a strange, new cage, all on her own.

Every day, the little
girl took her out. She
called her Fluffy and
stroked her. She was
kind, but she was not
like Molly's friends,
Jolly and Polly.

Sometimes Molly saw the little girl
playing with her own friends. This
made Molly feel sad.

And sometimes Mum and Dad peered in
at her, sighed and shook their heads.
They knew Molly was miserable.

Back in the petshop, Jolly and Polly were also feeling miserable. Life was no fun without their old friend, Molly.

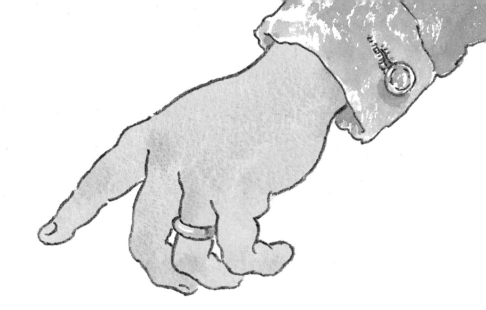

They were so sad, they did not notice
the customer until it was too late.
"That one, please," he said.

Suddenly, Mr Jones lifted Polly out of
the cage. She was very frightened.

Poor Jolly. Now she had lost both
her friends!

She was still sadly lying there when
Mr Jones reached down again.

"I've got just the one for you,
madam," he said . . .

"Come and look at Fluffy," said Dad.
"I had this great idea."

"Guess what?" laughed Mum. "So did I!"

Molly showed Jolly and Polly around
their new home. What fun they were
going to have here!

Now the three friends didn't have
to worry about customers any more.
They would be together forever.